A NOTE TO PARENTS

When your children are ready to "step into reading," giving them the right books—and lots of them—is as crucial as giving them the right food to eat. **Step into Reading Books** present exciting stories and information reinforced with lively, colorful illustrations that make learning to read fun, satisfying, and worthwhile. They are priced so that acquiring an entire library of them is affordable. And they are beginning readers with an important difference—they're written on four levels.

Step 1 Books, with their very large type and extremely simple vocabulary, have been created for the very youngest readers. **Step 2 Books** are both longer and slightly more difficult. **Step 3 Books,** written to mid-second-grade reading levels, are for the child who has acquired even greater reading skills. **Step 4 Books** offer exciting nonfiction for the increasingly proficient reader.

Children develop at different ages. **Step into Reading Books,** with their four levels of reading, are designed to help children become good—and interested—readers *faster.* The grade levels assigned to the four steps—preschool through grade 1 for Step 1, grades 1 through 3 for Step 2, grades 2 and 3 for Step 3, and grades 2 through 4 for Step 4—are intended only as guides. Some children move through all four steps very rapidly; others climb the steps over a period of several years. These books will help your child "step into reading" in style!

Library of Congress Cataloging-in-Publication Data:
Hautzig, Deborah. Happy Mother's Day! ; featuring Jim Henson's Sesame
Street Muppets / by Deborah Hautzig ; illustrated by Normand Chartier.
p.   cm.–(Step into reading. Step 1 book) SUMMARY: Grover is distressed
that he has no present to give his mother for Mother's Day, not realizing
that she already has the best present of all. [1. Mother's Day–Fiction.
2. Gifts–Fiction. 3. Puppets–Fiction] I. Chartier, Normand, ill. II. Children's
Television Workshop. III. Title. IV. Series.   PZ7.H288Has   1989
[E]–dc19 88-14002
ISBN: 0-394-82204-8 (pbk.); 0-394-92204-2 (lib. bdg.)

Manufactured in the United States of America   6 7 8 9 0

STEP INTO READING is a trademark of Random House, Inc.

Step into Reading

Happy Mother's Day!

Featuring Jim Henson's Sesame Street Muppets

by Deborah Hautzig

illustrated by Normand Chartier

A Step 1 Book

Random House/Children's Television Workshop

4

Sunday was Mother's Day!
Everyone in Grover's class
was making cards.

Grover cut out a red heart.

He put pink sparkles on it.

"What gift shall I give
my wonderful mommy?"
asked Grover.
"I will ask my friends."

"Give her a bunch
of stinkweed!"
said Oscar.

"No, my mommy
does not like stinkweed,"
said Grover.

"Give her a nice
new mop!" said Bert.

"Give her a rubber duckie!"
said Ernie.

14

"No, those are not
good gifts for a mommy,"
said Grover.

"I will ask Big Bird."

"Give her a birdseed cake,"
said Big Bird.

"No, my mommy is not
a bird," said Grover.
"I will ask Cookie Monster."

"Give cookies!"

said Cookie Monster.

"No, my mommy bakes
the best cookies
in the world,"
said Grover.

19

Grover walked home slowly.
"Oh, dear. I still do not have
a gift for my mommy,"
he said.

Grover's mother came out
to look for him.
"Grover, dear! Why are
you so sad?" she asked.

"This card is all
I have to give you
for Mother's Day,"
Grover said.

"What a lovely card,"

said his mother.

"But I do not have
a gift for you,"
said Grover sadly.

"Oh yes, you do,"
said his mother.

"YOU are my
Mother's Day gift.
If I did not have
my little Grover,
I would not be
a mother!"

Grover gave his mother
a big hug.

31

"Happy Mother's Day,"
said Grover.